I dedicate this book to the people who believed in me

and to those who has an amazing imagination

Boy of one, with souls of three-Book 1

Part one-Chapter one

August 12th 2010-7.45pm

Dear Diary,

This is the first time I have ever done this so let me start by telling you that my name Elliot and I am 16 years old. My hair is a very dark brown, almost black and my eyes are some kind of blue/grey. When I was about 14 years old, I wasn't very tall but since the summer holidays I have grown to nearly 6 foot 1. I am not really into anything sporty but that's probably because my dad isn't either, he is more of a computer nerd type of guy. I am kind of lucky considering I can see my dad whenever I like as he works from home, so whenever I need anything that is kind of a bonus. My mum definitely wears the trousers in our house, always trying to tell me what to do and that's the only reason I have this diary in the first place. Lucky for me, I am not an only child so some of that bossiness is mainly focused on my younger brother. He has everything; he gets what he wants and can do anything. When I mean he can do anything I mean, he is great at all the things I am not good at, such a sport. In a way I am kind of jealous but I guess I have that bond with my dad as I love computers too. Mainly computer games, but that's the same thing really.

Then there is finally, my twin baby sisters; they are 3 years old so I don't have to engage with any girly conversations at all, but to be honest by the time that will happen I will out of here. Even though they scream most of the time, they are kind of cute. I mean most babies are but they are identical which is kind of freaky because they are just clones of each other and whatever one of them does, the other one does exactly the same.

The only reason I am using this brown leather diary is because my mum is worried and thought I should write to you, and even though I think this is lame here I am. I don't want to bore you with all the details of my life but I just want to focus on telling you one, slightly odd adventure my life is turning out to be.

Diary I need to tell you that Bedtime is his time. I hate bedtime. The worst part of the day is when I have to go to sleep. When I'm nervous and scared I always feel itchy and just scratch at my skin till it feels good. But when its bedtime my brain always tells me I need to wash; just scrub my skin clean. It's now night time, but I don't want to go, so I'm just sitting in my bath scrubbing away at the dead flesh on my arms but then I begin to hear the tapping. Above my bath there's a dome shaped window on the ceiling. That small square window is the only freedom for light. The tapping happens on top of the window and when I hear it I hate to look above my head. My worst fear is tapping away, I try not to look but it's one of those things when you have to. As I look up I can see the skin crawling black bird tapping away with its orange beak. The tapping is the sign to tell me to go sleep as he's waiting for me. Slowly changing to my pyjamas it's time to go to sleep. Entering my dark room I quickly jump into bed so the others can't catch my feet from under the bed and keep me there forever.

My bed is placed in the middle of my room, my walls are blue and my curtains are blue. To the right of my bed I have built in wardrobes with two doors; that's where he lives. No matter how many times I try to escape him he always finds a way. Sleepovers at my house, sleepovers at my friend's house, sleeping with the light on, no matter what I do he finds me. One time when I left the light on I thought I was ok but as soon as I closed my eyes the lights turn off and he whispers my name.

The end, Elliot.

August 14th 2010-7.09pm

Dear Diary,

He is ruining my life. He's the people watcher. Waiting anxiously in
the hospital waiting room I glanced around the room to see so many
people treating this situation as a joke. It's Friday night and the room
is full of young and old and pretenders. I can only assume that people
like the feeling of feeling wanted and have people feeling sorry for
them just so they get some attention for the night but when the critical
patients need to be seen they just have to wait in line like everybody
else.

Entering the room I noticed three girls all dressed up looking as
though they were about to enjoy an alcohol fun filled evening but one
of the girls was sitting in a wheelchair waiting to be seen. Now not
ever breaking a bone or badly injuring myself before and correct me if
I'm wrong but you wouldn't be sitting there with a smile on your face
having a good chat with your friends while your leg supposedly hurts.
The worst pain I have probably experienced would have to be have
my ears pierced at the top of my ear and the after pain was horrible so
why was this girl not in pain? A faker perhaps?

What this girl should have planned was if she wanted attention she
would at least make her pain known so that maybe the two guys
sitting close by would talk to her? Now I watched these two young
guys swagger their way through the hospital, one with a ridiculous hat
on his head which remarkably reminded me of a sick bucket we
would get at school, the other guy was arguing with his friend over
the fact he didn't even need to be here but with not much persuasion
they remained in the waiting room. Trying to examine with my eyes
which one was the patient neither one really showed any pain, instead
they just relaxed making conversation, laughing and joking.

Being here for almost two hours I didn't even realise that a scruffy
looking girl was asleep on the chair. She was camouflaged to the chair

but made herself known by raising her arm in the air. A police officer approached her and asked her to leave but after pretending to disappear again she soon returned back to the chairs.

With us all waiting patiently to be seen another hour went by and an old gentleman joined the room in bright orange trousers on his electric wheelchair. Not saying a word he approached the coffee machine and then disappeared outside again but only to reappear asking for change of a£5 note to buy himself more coffee.

Now judging the room all I see is a group of people who needs are not as serious as why I am here. I am not hurt myself but my friend who I am with has her crisp white top stained in her own blood from her face. Her nose is bent and broken, her eye are bloodshot and bruised, she can barely move her left arm and her legs don't want to walk, but without making a fuss she sat there and waited. After nearly 4 hours she was finally seen.

After a while I was asked to join my friend in another room where they did some more tests. What happened to her was unexplainable, but to me I know who did it. It was him; the man in the cupboard. So the whole point of this diary was to explain to god what had happened while he wasn't here to sort this mess, as an innocent girl, my girlfriend, was pushed down the stairs. I believe in karma but she had done nothing to deserve this so with no explanation I have decided that my belief in god no longer exists, because the man in my room can't be stopped. Do you have any idea how it feels to see the person you love get hurt right in front of your eyes and have nobody there to help you. So god this diary entry is for you to keep and keep reading to see what a mess of this world you have made. I admit we all have made mistakes but knowing you have hurt someone I really care about and finally realise he's the one you have made me lose faith in you. This girl has always been there for me through all the bad stuff that's been done and to repay her you have damaged her body and her life.

You're sincerely,

No longer a believer.

Chapter Two

August 30th 2010- 6.55pm

Dear Diary,

Its time for me to tell you about him. Every time I go into my room to sleep he refuses to let me. Hiding under my blue covers he always finds me, I squeeze my eyes tight to shut him out but he comes into my dark mind. This man I speak of does not have a name but he lives in my cupboard; his face shows no features, his body is just like any other man apart from he has a tail. His whole body is black apart from his tail which is red and pointy, I know it sounds like I'm describing the devil but I don't believe it's him.

Diary, this man does not speak but when his head moves as though he is talking there are speech bubbles that appear above his head. He is not a nice man but a creation of my soul. He makes me do things that I don't want to. He makes me hurt people that I do not know. I do not actually leave my house but when I close my eyes at night he swallows me into his world and sends me to houses I have never seen. The first time this happened was at a young couple's house; I sat outside and watched them live. Until he decided it was time I had to go into their house and knock them out. While they were unconscious I hooked them to a needle and drained their bodies' dry of blood. Sometimes, just sometimes they would wake up half way through. This one time this man was so terrified, his eyes just stared into my soul but he was too weak to move. So I admit it, this is what I'm made to do, I have to take the blood from people but at the moment I don't even know what he wants it for. This is why my friend was hurt because he wanted her blood but I refused so instead he hurt her.

My eyes used to be a lovely, weird sort of colour but now my eyes just look like a panda because they are tired as I can no longer sleep. Diary, I am so tired of this,

Please help me.

September 9th 2010- 7.21pm

Dear Diary,

Last night has been very weird for me, because there was no tapping and he didn't come into my head. I actually had a full night's sleep. Should I be worried? I am not sure whether he is planning something big or whether he has found a better employee. In a strange way I feel betrayed that he has not even said a word to me, why am I feeling like this diary? This is not normal.

My first proper night's sleep was amazing; I never knew how comfortable my pillow was. I didn't even wake up once and the only thing that made me jump was hearing the sound of my alarm clock. I could definitely get used to this, but I am definitely changing my alarm tone. Speak soon, Elliot.

Is he back?

January 2nd 2012-5.14pm

Dear Diary,

I need to apologise because it's been so long since I have spoken to you but I felt I was fine because I don't see him anymore. It's like I scared him away and for a while I was sad about that but I got over it, I believe I scared him away because the last time I ever saw him was at my friend's house when he tried to force me to take his blood but I said no!

Diary, the reason I am writing to you again is because something does not feel right. I am now 18 years old, so that technically makes me an adult, well kind of, but I wanted you to know that I'm frightened. Before I tell you what has happened I just want to introduce you to someone so special to me. Her name is Wendy, I have known her for a long time but now she is finally my girlfriend. She is the most sweetest, kindest person I know.

The other day, I was leaving my Girlfriend's house and the drive home is always horrible at night because it's a long bendy road with trees and more trees either side. I remember when I was younger I used to always look at the trees when I was in the car with my dad driving somewhere at night and I always looked out the window just in case I saw someone. I never did though. Anyway, on the way home my lights on the car focused on movement in the trees as I was turning a corner and out of nowhere a dark figure appeared with a shovel. Do you think it's him, diary?

E.

January 3rd 2013-10.15pm

Dear Diary,

The night I told you that I saw him well to be truthful and I am afraid to admit it was him. I know it had been two years since I last spoke to you but that night was the worst night of my life and it's taken until now to tell you the truth.

The night where it appeared as though I saw a man on the side of the road was in fact him. This is so hard for me to tell you but when I saw this man with a shovel it was because the most terrible thing I can ever imagine to happen to me actually happened. That shovel was used to dig a shallow grave for my late girlfriend Wendy. That night when I was tucked up in bed sleeping, she was being dragged from her room and suffered a death that was highly unlikely peaceful. After he had done his achievement of another life taken he visited my room that very same night. I could feel his hot breath breathing behind me, and as I turned around he was standing there covered in blood and still had the shovel in his right hand. I felt suddenly sick and my heart shattered to so many tiny pieces you couldn't possibly stick them back together. Without him even telling me I just knew what he had done and to prove he wasn't lying he took me to where he buried her.

It was dark and the trees around me were green and scary in the moonlight. He pointed to the ground and there in front of me was her grave. He must have felt as though he owed it to me, by burying her as he usually gets rid of the bodies in disturbing ways. As I lay on the ground beside her, I could see her hand was not completely buried, so I held it for a while and imagined we were in her room laying on the bed listening to her favourite music, imagining the smell of her beautiful hair. But when reality hit me I began to cry and then my tears turned to anger and I screamed at him, asking him why did he do this? She has done nothing wrong! But he just stared at me watching me slowly die. I buried her hand with the rest of her body and he took me home.

For days I was distant from everyone, not telling a soul what had happened. I even had to cover up the fact that I knew about what had happened to her, so all I could do was lie to her friends and her family. Every time I lied to someone a dagger poked at my heart. My poor Wendy, I am so sorry.

Mentally scarred forever,

Elliot.

Dear diary,

I know this is a lot to take in for you, because believe me it's happening to me, but ever since I told you what had happened I feel as though a part of Wendy is inside of me and I kind of like it. Sometimes when I am on my own, she even talks to me and tells me not to worry about her as she will always be with me. At first, it freaked me out and I started to believe I was going crazy but then I had to except it, I have officially gone crazy. The man from my cupboard is still here and my life is only just beginning for real this time. I have decided to call him the shadow man as it is better than just calling him the man that lives in my cupboard. Diary, my life is about to get complicated I can feel my soul changing, but is it going to be good?

I am sorry if I don't get time to talk to you much now as I am going to busy for a while.

Speak to you real soon,

Love Elliot, Wendy & the shadow man.

Chapter Three

I could not cope without Wendy

I guess I never understood why Wendy was taken away from me, she was truly an angel. I have come to realise the pain of her going is something so painful I just cannot begin to describe. When our eyes met it was like the sun was rising over the ocean. When she smiled, goose bumps appeared all over my body. We were meant to be together.

As I look at her lovingly through the window I think to myself why she hasn't invited me in yet. I kept breathing talent all over the window, which was making it hard for me to see her. As I wiped away the hot breath, I could see an unfamiliar figure that was smeared in the room. I pressed my nose to the glass, she's cheating on me! How could she? As the tears ran down my face, they began to freeze, before they fell off my chin. I decided to run. I didn't know where I was going, but it definitely wasn't here.

Getting over the fact she maybe didn't love me anymore, I continued to watch them through the window every night; I couldn't sleep, eat or drink because of her. I just wanted to die after she broke my heart. One night she caught me watching her, I wanted to run but I just froze in the winter night. She came out with a confused look on her face and asked who I was. I felt shocked. 'What do you mean who am I? You know who I am stop pretending!' I screamed. With a soft and gentle voice she said 'are you okay?' my heart shattered into a thousand pieces just hearing her voice and feeling her warm touch on my arm.

I kept having these nightmares that she was murdered, with every detail that felt so real. I would wake up crying and when I looked beside me she wasn't there, but then I realise she's with him. Each night the same detailed dream plays through my mind and it never changes not even the slightest detail.

Everywhere in town I went, she was always there. As I watched her even more I noticed that the cute mole on her neck had gone. Seeing her everywhere really began to ruin my life. As I was eating in my favourite Italian restaurant she shows up with a stranger. Seriously? Why would she be here at my one special place? Our special place. As I ate alone, I kept looking over at her; she just wasn't the same person I thought she was. Her laugh echoed the room so loud it hurt my ears and then, I just lost it. Without thinking I grabbed my blunt knife stupidly and ran for the stranger she sat with. With a raised arm, I glanced at her. The only sound that echoed afterwards was her screams. I just couldn't do it. She came over to me and repeatedly asked "why do you keep following me and what is your problem?" I said "seriously? It's like I don't exist" a puzzled look filled her face.

Fourteen days later I sat back on the sofa ready for my next session. "Now, are you sure you're ready to tell me everything that happened that day and that you remember at any time you can stop" said the stranger on the chair in front of me.

'Yes, I remember, it was the day I returned home from her house after watching this scary film she has been waiting to watch.' All my memories flashed through my head and my tears couldn't help but run down my face. No words would leave my mouth so I sat there speechless. That girl I have been following around was not Wendy, just some girl that reminded me of her. How silly am I not to realise, I felt so embarrassed. I was like an obsessive stalker I was longing for this stranger to be her. For her to just smile and make things all better again. I just blocked everything that was bad out of my head. I hate myself for what I did, it just wasn't me.

Now the storm has passed

The boy of one with souls of three, lives a life of misery, one soul bad and one soul good, the one soul left just never understood. He killed to please the shadow man, killing as many girls as he can, he would cut off their hair to keep for treasure, while the shadow man keeps their souls for pleasure. The girl name Wendy is the second soul, to make the boy good is her goal, but as long as the shadow man controls them with his years, Wendy is going to face her fears. The boy of one with souls of three, is in love with a girl, but the others can't see, she's really special, with a name called penny, she has one soul, which isn't many, with these three souls he wants just one, he's got to choose; is it peace? Love? Or will he end it with a gun?

Chapter Four

Letting the painful sting roll down my cheeks was the only option I could think of right now. They told me to turn my life around or I could end up in the ground. But I just can't keep myself away; it gives me a sense of feeling alive. Smelling the dirty air tends to linger wherever I place my feet. He is such a loner, hiding himself away in that room, all day and all night. I remember seeing him always clutching this black book hard in his arms. Guarding it like it was his soul inside. Being young meant you might have yourself an imaginary friend, well he still has his. I see him talking to himself or someone all the time. He had no friends, nobody liked him and nobody ever talked to him. He was in a bubble, an amazing non-breakable bubble. Whenever he was alone with that sad pathetic look on his face, I would make him centre of attention, just to make him feel like he was worthy of something. 'Snip, Snip, snip' here we go with the scissors cutting away at the skin. 'Hack, hack, hacking' away till the poison runs free.

I know your motives, I can tell your plan. You are not a very good liar; your smile gives it away every time. You all know my name but you don't talk to me, I just see you all waiting for the right time to exploit me but I, I, I have it all written down you see? You can't deceive me not anymore. Especially Penny; her blonde wavy hair, those bright blue watery eyes cannot touch me. She is powerless, lifeless, and bloodless. I can still here the scratching on the door every time I close my damn eyes. "Please help me" she cried "Please let me go" she screamed. Who does she think she is? Penny it's too late now, you can no Longer deny your love, your lies, the fake that spread in your eyes. Sitting the other side of the door from her I whisper:

'Killing you was all so fun,
Now this taste has just begun,
Finding you was not hard,
If I don't kill you, your life will be scarred,
For the rest Keep one eye open just wait and see,
You all deserve this don't you see?
I know you exist; I know you're alive,
Shall we see if you can survive?'

This poem is my best one yet, I wonder if she will like it? I hope she does; maybe, just maybe her eyes will widen and join me in this little adventure of mine. "Wendy, Wendy?" my voice projects louder so she can hear me clearly. "Where are you? I know you are here, don't hide from me, why can't you see I just want to help you." Trying to find her secretly but the door creaked open, damn it, I need to fix this door. Clutching a pair of scissors her face catches mine. "There you are! What are you doing? You shouldn't do this, not really. We have a better plan now, remember?" the blank expression on her face says it all, I know she doesn't want to join, quite simply because she doesn't feel she has it in her but I know she does. She has to otherwise she will just be another one.

Staring at this monster we created is unforgiving, I have the scissors in my hand right, now I could do it this time, I really could, Oh, could I? Watching her watching me makes her nervous I can tell. Lifting my right hand she gently raises her left. "C'mon Wendy do it, cut me, I dare you" Her mouth spoke "you killed Penny so why shouldn't I kill you?"

Wendy is the angel in my head; well that is what I think she is now. I can feel her taking over my body sometimes but when unfortunate things happen to all of my girlfriends she blames me, although when it does happen, she forgives me and I thank her for that. My mother thought I was crazy when I told her That Wendy is with me, what a silly woman! How can she think her own son is crazy?

I don't want to do this again, but today I need to kill another one. Just going to cut open their chest and watch their heart slowly come to a stop. Then I'm going to cut a piece of their hair and add it to my book of heartbreakers. Twenty-seven now in total. When will they begin to learn? When will these women realise they can't have everything. Today a star is born, a killer.

The water sliding down my throat bubbled and came back up. I nearly had a coughing fit. My cat just sat there, staring at me. He didn't even care if I chocked and died. How dare he just stare?

I'm not going back there. Back to that padded room they locked me in. I thought I was going to die. I nearly thought I was going crazy but the voice in my head told me I was fine. I have already escaped from there once; I'm not doing it again. No way!

I thought she was the one person that wasn't going to break my heart. I bought Penny flowers every day and took her everywhere she wanted. But then one day she started missing my phones calls and I started seeing her with this man. He wasn't better looking than me, so what was she doing? Her hair is in my book now. It's stuck right on the middle page, her lovely long blonde hair.

The blood ran from her head to her chest, quickly as if it was water running from a tap. Then she fell to the ground screaming. The door just kept scratching and scratching and scratching until it suddenly stopped and everything went silent. I went completely deaf, but I couldn't stop staring at this one picture. Straight in front of me the picture was of a man and woman dancing on the beach, they looked so happy but of course it has to be picture perfect. As I stared at the picture I could see my reflection and then I felt one single tear, drop down my face and splash onto the floor. Then everything slowed down and my eyes went black.

I just couldn't stop her screams in my head that would constantly drown out the rest of the world. It was like she was inside my head and a video of it would be on replay. Just get out, get out of my head. But she won't listen. Just please listen to me, go away. I don't need you to be a constant reminder of the guilt. It was your fault. You shouldn't have left me.

I just got sick of the crying and heartbreak so I had to do something. I was at home one night on my own in the kitchen, looking through my little black book of achievements and something caught my eye. I was just staring at the sink, at something shiny. There was a small knife on the side. I picked it up and just stared at my reflection. I was disgusted with what I could see. I was so angry. I pulled up my sleeve and pierced the skin on my wrist and watched myself bleed. I felt a warm feeling as if it was love. I did it again and again till I started to feel weak, so I cleaned to the knife and went to my room and laid on my bed and felt the blood bleed through my sheets.

I can feel her breathing heavy across my face; a black shadow passes my eyes from right to left. I am terrified. I can feel my nose beginning to run but I am too scared to reach for a tissue. What is wrong with me? I am just paralyzed like she was. Light footsteps are wandering around my bed; I can feel their presence surrounding me, making me feel trapped. A cold breath begins to blow in my ear whispering my name, it was her. She has come back for me. I squeeze my eyes tighter but then I feel a cold hand touching my neck. I suddenly sneeze and I am sitting upright. The room is dark and cold, there is no one here but myself. I am back, back in that room again. How did they find me? I climbed out of bed and headed to the sink, and as I got closer I could see my reflection in the mirror. There is blood dripping from my nose and bloody hand marks on my neck. She tried to get me back.

Chapter Five

I sat at the table in my kitchen watching the candle flicker in front of me. The bright orange flame dances to the silent music that is being played. I put my hand to the flame so I can feel the heat, its power. Oh boy, it's hot! Putting the palm of my hand close, the flame goes out and darkness fills the room. I relight the candle and do it again and again and now my hand is black and burnt. I relight the candle a last time and this time it doesn't move, not even a flicker. I place my hand over the flame but I feel no heat. Someone is holding my hand and guarding the heat but there is nobody else here. I think he must have followed me, I can feel him watching my every move. I switch the Christmas lights on so that the tree can have time to shine but as I turned them on all the glass decorations suddenly fall to the floor and smash into such tiny pieces that they have hibernated in the carpet.

The shadow man has contacted me again. His ghostly presence always sends chills down my spine. His appearance is black: no face, no features, just a shadow of the night and his red tail. He told me the time was coming near and I need to prepare for what might be the end. He has promised me fame, fortune and everything I could possibly ever wish for just as long as I serve his needs and complete this mission from God. Wendy doesn't like him, she doesn't like it when he interferes in our life, but I like him. Wendy didn't know about the shadow man and what he was like before I knew her. He used to cut my arms dry to free the sin of the devil that lay inside. But one day when the shadow man came into my room he told me to prepare myself for the journey and said to me:

"I need you to cut yourself. I want you to slice your arms. Make sure you do it downwards and not across otherwise you won't get the better high than you normally would. I am going to need you do it and you need to do it slow, so I can watch the blood pour off your arm and trickle all over mine, so that it soaks into my skin and become mine. When you start to feel as though you're almost going to die, tell me, so you can stop and I can help you with the tricky part. I will sew your arms back up so you're all good as new."

Now at first I didn't know what to expect but I trusted the man, well to be honest I was a little scared of him. When I did it I never felt so alive, something changed me that day but whatever it was gave me a thirst for more.

When I finally thought I met the second love of my life I was wrong again. Penny was the one for me until the shadow man proved me wrong. He convinced me to go to the coffee shop down the avenue and there she was with another man. I knew that today was going to be the happiest day of my life so far and I was just so nervous to do it but I knew it was right. There she was looking all lovely with her hair flowing straight past her shoulders staying perfectly still. She looked like an angel just walking towards me. Hello she said to me in her voice, which made me shiver and give me that butterfly feeling in my stomach. But oh dear Penny, this doesn't look good does it? I was going to ask you to be my wife, to make my life complete, to be mine forever and always. But you ripped my heart out of my chest and left it pounding on the floor till it stopped, and then crumbled to so many pieces I couldn't possibly be able to mend it. Now my heart doesn't beat anymore. I took her back to my place and that was when the magic happened in the cupboard. Thinking about it, those scratch marks are never going to disappear from the door.

Remembering what happened that day as I lay in my bed, it was quite an eventful day, I got my revenge in the end, even though that was never really what I wanted to happen, I wanted to be happy just like any normal person but clearly I was not supposed to be normal. God gave me this as a purpose in life not to be happy but to hurt her like she did to me.

Now that Penny has gone, my journey has begun, my taste for blood has become real and I thirst for more. I see a lot more of the shadow man than I do Wendy now. I miss her; I hope she hasn't left me for good.

There are no limits to what I would do. Sitting outside this woman's house hiding, was like a breath of fresh air. I could smell her blood from here and I haven't even seen her face yet. Parked on the road, listening to my favourite music, oncoming cars are blinding me with their white lights. Each flash of heaven, darts through my eyes. He is watching, waiting for me to begin this one.

Biting my bottom lip I can see she's entered her bedroom. I can see you. Her room has now darkened and this is my queue to count to thirty minutes before I make my move. Oh I am ever so excited. The waiting and the planning is always such a thrill of a possibility that I could get caught but I never do. I wonder if anyone has even heard of me yet.

Chapter Six

Jesus was a good man, he was loved and worshipped but only had 12 followers. Hitler was hated yet he was loved. The people who worshipped him believed the things he was doing and what he did to people were right. He had so many followers. I want to be like him, I'm going to be in his shoes. Now, if Jesus was generally a good man, then why did he let such hurtful things happen to me and why is he so special. He may be the son of God, but aren't we all. For me they believe that there is a God he has to be two people in one. To elaborate on my opinion if he truly is a good man he must also be the devil inside too. my explanation is that God cannot be all good, because he punishes the bad by sending them to hell therefore he too is not nice because if he was good then everyone would go to heaven regardless whether they did right on earth or not.

Sitting on the roof of my house I sat there gazing at the stars talking to the shadow man; the fallen angel of god was my friend. I believe that he could be a good being; he takes all the people who have done wrong in the world back to his kingdom of hell. He is god of the underworld; he rescues all of the bad people and takes them to hell so they are not punished on earth for their wrongdoings. He told me that I am not ready to see the heaven of the underworld, just not yet. I am his little protégée on earth, to cause all the hell on earth to make earth into a new underworld for his people. He describes hell to me, which is just how the bible tells us; full of fire. He wants all the girls who have done wrong to live in his castle and serve him for eternity which is what I am here on earth to do. I find all the women who have done wrong and take their lives to live in a better world.

From the age of 7 I went to therapy classes twice a week; Monday and Thursday. I would talk and she would listen. All I did was talk; I spoke about my friend Wendy and then I would make things up about real life monsters. She used to think I was crazy and one time when I was 12 years old I believed the monster had bit her ear, but she accused me and I never returned there. March 24th 2005, I remember that day so well. I was watching cartoons and eating prawn cocktail crisps and the doorbell rang. I must have shouted to mum about 5 times before she even reached to the door. 12.32pm and these three men dressed in white coats came and had a talk with me, although they talked I don't recall a single word they said as I was just focusing on the rabbit being chased on the TV. Within an hour of them leaving my mum went upstairs filled a suitcase and with tears down her eyes she put me in the car. Refusing to do so twice, in the end she had the get the next door neighbour to carry me into the car. I was hell. As soon as they put on my seatbelt I undone it and ran out the other side of the car. I remember being so frightened like a little boy all alone in the dark.

Love? What is love? The definition of love to me is an emotion of affection and personal attachment. Now love has not been a stranger to me, I have loved many but attachment worries me. What if I get too attached, even so that I just won't be able to do it?

Commitment? I find it hard to commit to just one person in a relationship since Wendy left, yet I don't have a problem with commitment because I used to do that. It's my obligation to commit to the secret pleasure of taking one's life.

On the night of the 23rd of April, the showers outside were pouring and flooding my garden. As I sat at my table in the dining room I was trying to read the newspaper but I couldn't concentrate with that noise of the rain, it felt like someone was continuously poking me in the head trying to get my attention. With the unbearable noise of the rain I tried to read the newspaper to see if anyone had recognised my work, suddenly the music box in the corner of the room sitting on the top shelf of my book case began to play a haunting tune. The fairy on the toad stool sitting under a pink flower was singing a tune but this music box has not been wound up for almost 3 years. Princess of the poppies was a warning that it's time again.

When I get the chance I like to go to my local pub for a drink just to watch the drunks make complete fools of themselves. This was a perfect opportunity. Of course I don't drink I just stick to lemonade. In the corner of the room by the bar, is my favourite spot and an eye catching view of the beauty serving my drinks. Now I'm not sure whether it is fortunate or unfortunate that today is all about herself. With a flicker of the light and a tug at my book his signal was made clear. As I sat and watch the locals attempt to pathetically chat her up she catches me. Oh that shiver of pure filth flew down my spine. Staring into each other's eyes forgetting the rest of the world she approaches me and asks if I would like a refill of my drink. As we chatted for the next two hours it was getting near to closing time. I headed for the toilet to hide and when everyone left, you could hear the clinking of the glasses as the beauty collected and tidied. A turn of a key of the cellar, I made my move. Step by step she went down further till when she got inside I appeared at the top of the stairs. I could see her jump of her skin when I smashed the door wide open and as she turned she smiled and said I scared her. I returned the smile and headed down to eye level. Without a word she put her arms round me and began to kiss me. I pushed her gently to the floor and smashed a bottle open with the glass flying into her face. Little cuts on her face made the blood flow slowly down her cheeks. She was scared, frightened and quiet; however I was excited and thrilled.

I bent down and licked the blood off her face. I smashed her over the head to knock her out, and then I reached into my pocket and got out the hammer and nails. This girl was special to shadow man he quite liked this girl as she was pure and honest inside and out. Picking her up by her feet I nailed them to the wall so she appeared to be hanging upside down. Grabbing her left hand, I stretched out her arm and hammered her hand with her fingers spread apart and then did the same with the right. The thirsty work was done so I drank a bottle of lemonade and watched the blood from her body go straight to her head and just when she was waking up I stabbed a nail in her forehead so she couldn't say a word. Her body has been nailed just like Saint Peter to make her unworthy of Jesus but to shadow man.

Chapter Seven

Wendy to me is now a white angel of heaven; she's so kind and forgiving. Her long red hair flows perfectly past her shoulders and flicks at the end making it look bouncy. I miss smelling the fruity smell of her hair once she has washed it, but sometimes when I am at home, I can smell her for just a second. Her eyes are blue pools of lush cold water. Her heavenly smile brightens my day after working so hard for the shadow man. She's so perfect in every way that I just want to please her but she won't let me, she wants to please me and care for me but I can't allow her to do so.

We used to have such great journeys together when she was actually still alive and we both had a dream of having a huge family and live in a massive house, with a swimming pool and our very own boat. But now, these memories of mine will never come true unless they are with someone else.

I can always tell it's her when she is here, by the clinking of her heels on the ground. The key ring chain attached to her bag makes a metal sound when it hits her hip after every step she takes. One day when she was sat with me alone without the shadow man she tried to talk some sense into me and tell me that the shadow man is not a nice person. The words she spoke was inspiring and stuck on the wall in black and white in my head and when I am in that stage of trying to get to sleep at night it would sometimes flash before my eyes to remind me of these words. The words she spoke were:

"I am not much of a believer of the any faith but seeing people being punished should not happen. Why do people kill people? The overall achievement may be a little satisfaction that lasts a second but doesn't the guilt build up inside so much that you either have a taste to go mental and kill more or you believe that almighty god will guide you and replenish your sins from evil. To be able to go that far as to grab hold of that gun and pull that trigger is astonishingly disgusting, looking into that persons eyes and see the soul of that life vanish in a second, doesn't that make you want to pull that same trigger on yourself? People need to wake up and see that fighting with each other solves nothing, it just creates more anger and more reason to retaliate until that moment is gone and nobody knows why we are doing it. I want to be able to make a difference in this life I have, to make you aware that violence is a sin and it achieves absolutely nothing. It does not make you worthy, loved and admired but hated and even go as far as loathed. You are not special using a gun or a weapon for that matter. If you want something in life you must work for it, with blood sweat and tears and if I can manage to help you and change you then I know I have done something right. Please don't listen to that man anymore. Learn from what he did to me please, I love you always."

As those words repeat in my mind over and over again I can't help but think that she is right. I need to sort my life out. Maybe I should get a nice girlfriend and start my life new. On the TV I keep seeing these adverts for online dating so I might give that a go just to make Wendy happy and see if I can change for her.

How can you justify that you like someone without face to face interaction? Surely there's no chemistry there until your eyes meet for that very first time and you communicate with words and gestures. When your skin brushes each other for the first time even if it was for a second you would know when the shivers run down your spine and the hairs on the back of your neck stand up. I do not believe you can truly like someone online? Can you?

I have been talking to this young girl; just turned 20, long black, curly hair, brown eyes and a pretty smile. I can tell by her pictures she is a lot of fun, I think the best photo of her is the one where she is waving at the person behind the camera while she is on the tea cups at a theme park. She looks so happy and full of life.

We chatted for about a week and then I popped the big question and asked if she would like to go for coffee, within minutes she simply replied YES! All in capitals as if she shouted it to me with excitement. Hmm what to wear? I could go casual; jeans and a top or jeans and a shirt? I need to discuss this with Wendy, she will always give me a good honest opinion and plus she is a woman with taste and knows what a girl wants. With many arguments and disagreements we decided to go with grey jeans, black top and a black jumper.

So the day of the date arrives and my hands are sweaty, and I am sitting nervously at the table hoping she will show up. Ten whole minutes went by and when the door opened I just knew it was her by the sound of her footsteps, it must be her. She approached my table and with a grin and a hello she sat down. Wearing a black skirt and a red top I have never seen anything so beautiful, well beautiful now. I mean I will never forget Penny, or my sweet darling Wendy. Laughing and conversation flowing there was no awkward silences. We talked for so long that without even realising the day outside turned to night. Leaving the café I gave her a hug and a kiss on the cheek and with that she departed leaving me with a promise of a phone call later, and a much promised second date. I watched her walk away with her hair swinging from side to side and I couldn't help but have a taste for blood.

Lingering behind her, hiding behind cars and bins as I followed her down the road she must have walked for a mile before she finally reached some steps and headed up to her flat door. Watching from behind a wall I watched her walk in and lucky for me her door was the very first flat. Peering through her window, I watched her pour a glass of red wine; first glass and then a second and suddenly I'm making my move. Pressing the button for door number 3 I waited patiently for her answer. 'Hello' she questioned, I froze and couldn't say a word. 5 seconds went by and she buzzed me in. Is she really that idiotic by letting anyone in? Silly girl.

So I approached her door and with her door left ajar I crept my way inside. I closed the door silently and made my way to her kitchen. Before she could even turn to recognise her killer I grabbed her hands, lifted them behind her back so she couldn't move. 'Who are you?' she cried with panic and fear. I said nothing and moved her hair off her neck kissing her and as I was doing that I pulled her right arm up higher till it clicked out of the socket. With one hand I grabbed her hair and smashed her head against the kitchen side knocking her asleep.

I lifted her left arm slipping that out of place till her arms were lifeless. Out of my jacket pocket comes my hammer, nails and this time some rope. Hammering the nails in her hands I tie the rope to the nails to control her like a puppet. Searching her flat I find a box full of sewing needles and cotton. With her lips sewn shut I painted her face with makeup and oh she looks so beautiful.

I sat her on the chair and I sat on the table behind her. 'Hello everyone' I made her say using her left hand to wave. She is such fun, maybe I should take her home to play with on rainy days? I am sure the shadow man will like her. UH OH what about Wendy? Oh I forgot about her she is not going to like this.

Chapter Eight

The boy of one, with souls of three,
There's some words to come out of me,
So I have this confession that I need to make,
penny isn't dead but she is awake,
I lied to the shadow man Indeed I did,
But my love I just couldn't get rid,
I just put her to sleep,
For no more than a week,
But when she's awake,
I just hope for her sake,
That the boy of one, with souls of three,
All disappears and what's left will be me.

I have laid Penny's body so beautifully on the single bed in my spare room. For her to wake up, it would be with truth loves kiss, like the fairy tale. Although I try not to admit to myself that I am still scared of the shadow man but I am, and I am not sure when is the right time for me to wake her and start my life with her. I want to make my life worth living; I need to somehow get rid of his soul that is inside of me but how? I remember learning in school of exorcism but I doubt that is even real and seeing films about it only frightens me more.

For a week or so, I sat thinking in my room of how I am going to do this, but every time a plan comes to mine it always uses violence but I guess that's the only way? The most difficult part of my plans is having to come to terms with the fact that if violence is used then I am going to suffer because the shadow man's soul lies inside of me so I would have to rip him out by hurting myself. If this is indeed to case I am going to prepare myself and be brave just so I can see Penny again.

When the shadow man was silent in my body I had time to tell Wendy my plan and I apologised for the fact that I am going to have to use violence to get what I have always secretly wanted; to be in love with someone and live with them forever. Although in my mind I always thought it was going to be Wendy but I know that now it will never happen so Penny is my last chance to love someone again. Wendy was very understanding and told me if that what it takes then she accepts the danger I am getting myself into and that when the shadow man is gone she will pass onto heaven and will live the rest of her days watching me be happy.

It has been almost a month after I had told Wendy my plan and tonight it was going to finally happen for real. With the shadow man living and breathing inside me I could feel his soul getting stronger with the amount of souls he has stolen from innocent bodies. 'Shadow man we need to talk' I said to myself looking in the mirror. As his face appears in front of me I told him it was time to leave and let me move on but he refused to believe this was my idea and started to blame Wendy. He suddenly became

Very aggressive, demanding that Wendy shows her face so that he can get rid of her, so that her words are no longer an influence of mine. Luckily, she stayed out of it and she never showed her face.

But I began to shout at him, showing no mercy. 'It has nothing to do with Wendy, I thought of this all on my own and I should of had the courage to do so when you took the love of my life away and then tried to do the same with Penny, but I am not going to let this happen any longer, so you have to go' without hesitation I raised the knife and stabbed it straight into my heart. I felt the cold of the knife in my body and the shadow man disappeared from the mirror. Feeling my body turn weak I leant over Penny and kissed her so her freedom was alive again.

With no movement of her body, I felt mine getting weaker and weaker and the blood began to pour even more. I slowly fell to the ground and as my eyes began to close, I could hear Wendy's voice telling me 'I Love You'

The final chapter

Just when I thought my plan had failed, which lead me to believe I have instead taken my life, I awoke in a place which can only be described as the in-between before you go to heaven. This place is cold and lonely and all I can think about is wondering whether I will ever get to see Wendy again. I know I will still have Penny but I cannot stress enough that Wendy will always be the one for me.

I felt as though I had been wondering around in this place for days. Everywhere was grey and mysterious, and no matter how far I walked I have not seen a soul or for that matter even heard the shadow man. Clutching my chest, it feels empty. I hope that the emptiness is because the shadow man has gone, but in my mind I don't think he will ever leave me.

Wondering around for days, I think my mind is starting to lose it. In the distance I can see Wendy for real this time, she is dressed in her favourite black dress and she is skipping towards me with that great big smile on her face. I started to head towards her and as I reach out to touch her she disappears into thin air. I rub my eyes to try and wake up from this nightmare but I then begin to see Penny in the same dress, running towards me. I try not to get disappointed so I just watch her, and as she gets to my face, she blows a kiss and vanishes.

Holding my head, I screamed as loud as I could but no one can hear me, not anymore. I lay on the ground, staring into the greyness above and I can hear my sisters singing and laughing but when I look they are nowhere to be seen. What is happening to me? I don't like this anymore.

I just want this nightmare to end but it won't go away. I just want to be with my family, safe at home but that is never going to happen now. I have probably killed myself and so forever I will be here alone with the pretend people scrambling my mind.

I have lost count of how long I think I have been here but I can tell it feels like it has been months. These people who keep wondering around no long disappears when I go near them, instead when I try to touch them my hand just goes straight through. These people here do not do a lot; they just walk around like zombies waiting as though they are waiting for me to go. But go where? I have no clue. This one time it actually felt as though Wendy's hand touched mine, but maybe it was just my mind playing tricks on me.

All the searching and too much thinking is making me very tired. Am I ever going to escape here, or is this my punishment. I decided to lay on the cold, damp floor, so I can rest my eyes for a bit, but all I can here is Wendy's voice telling me 'I Love you'

I suddenly woke from my sleep to the sound of machines beeping. I guess I am no longer alone. Too afraid that it was one of the shadow man's sick plans, I couldn't open my eyes and instead I just said 'Hello?' and with a response I knew so familiar replied 'Elliot it's me, your finally awake, open your eyes, it's me!' but before I opened my eyes I began to think I must be in heaven or possibly hell because that voice was Wendy.

Without too much thinking and sudden bravery, I opened my eyes and there she was. Wendy has never looked so beautiful. 'It's really you' I screamed with excitement. A puzzled, yet happy look appeared on her face and she told me that she has been with me every single day that I have been here. I can only assume she means, in my soul. 'How long have I been here' I asked, and with that she replied three months.

Three whole months of being here! Really, she must have this all wrong? I was completely shocked and confused, because it only seemed like yesterday that I stabbed myself and to add to this confusion Wendy is meant to be dead. 'Am I actually alive, because your meant to be dead, I am so confused' I asked her and with such sweet sadness that filled her face she asked me if I knew why I was her in the first place? I told her that I stabbed myself to let him go free and for you to be at peace. Instead of agreeing, she shook her head. Trying to act as though everything was ok, even though I could tell she was thinking I was being weird, she took my hand, stroked it and explained.

She told me that I had been really sick for a while, and the doctors believed I had schizophrenia, because of all the non-stop personalities and weirdness. I refused to believe this so I lifted my top to prove I am right, but when I looked down to see my heart, there wasn't even a scar. Tears began to fill my eyes and she cuddled me tight and told me I was better and that I could go back home with her. I squeezed her back and closed my eyes 'Never leave me' I whispered to her. 'I will never leave you' she replied.

I heard the door open, so I quickly opened my eyes to see if it was the rest of my family; My mum, my dad, my brother and my two sisters, but as I looked up at the door, it was Penny. 'Penny, what are you doing here?' I said in a quiet voice. Before her mouth could open, Wendy said 'don't be silly, Penny is the nurse who has been looking after you and been keeping me company' I started to feel confused again, what is actually going on. 'Hello stranger' Penny said as she filled up my water cup. 'I bet you had a nice long sleep, I hope you're ready to get back out there in the big wide world again!' she smiled. 'Um yes, I guess so' I replied.

My head began to feel dizzy and I thought I was going to be sick. My head touched the pillow again and my eyes closed. When I opened them again, Penny had gone but left me a jug of water and a sandwich on my tray. Beside me was Wendy, who was holding my hand telling me to wake up. I reassured her that I was ok and it was just so much confusion and information to take in but I finally feel ok. She showed me those big white teeth and got up and sat on my bed. She adjusted my bed so I was sitting upright with her.

We looked into each other's eyes and I never felt so happy and I can tell she is so happy that I am ok. She began to cry but only with happiness. I pulled her in close and told her that everything is ok now. I held onto her until I knew she was ok, but before I let her go the door opened again. I looked up in hope that this time it was my family, but instead, walking towards me with a knife in his hand, was the shadow man.

The boy of one, with souls of three,

Used to live a life of misery,

With too many souls, his head couldn't cope,

So he came up with a plan, and began to hope,

He sacrificed his life, but did he succeed?

Or did the shadow man, just make him bleed,

The stab in the heart, made him free his soul,

Or was it a trick, did the shadow man reach his goal,

For is he still here? Buried deep inside,

Maybe Elliot, just wished he should had died,

For this secret makes him crazy, but what can he do?

Was he even real, was he even true?

This is a story, which I will leave with you,

So YOU can decide, as I bid you adieu

The End, or is it.

Book Two-Chapter One

The Man in the shadow

Being on death row for 3 years, he no longer feared what was in store for him after he died. On the day of the electric chair, he had his last meal which consisted of a rare blooded steak and thick cut chips, smothered in peppercorn sauce. With a belly full, he was carefully tied to the chair. The room where you could watch him suffer, was full of the families of the mothers/daughters/sisters that he took away. With nothing left to say, justice began to take place. As everyone watched his body vigorously shake, he began to froth at the mouth. Believing he was dead, they stopped the machine. Before they were about to untie his body, he starting coughing up all the nastiness that he choked on. Everyone in the watching room gasped in horror. How on earth did that man survive?

Trying to figure out what went wrong the prison guards decided to try something different. There was a new lethal injection and he was going to be the first person to try it out, even though there was a slight possibility it would not work. On the day it was decided to happen, he got another last meal and more people turned up to watch him die. Tied to the chair again, they injected his body with the poison. No longer than a minute later, blood started to pour out of his nose, mouth and ears. His body started to shake and his eyes went black. All those who witnessed this death all admitted that it looked as though his soul left his body and went into a dark shadow in the corner of the room. Some of them say that when his soul left into the shadows they could still hear his bone shivering laugh. To be certain of his death, they burnt his body till there was nothing left but dust. Thus, the shadow man was born.

Before the shadow man even existed, he belonged to a body of a being which should not be described as human. The man was a bit of a lady lover, but his love for them was beyond extreme. Once he had finished with one he would cut a piece of their hair, stick it in his black book, then he would kill them. His taste of this wickedness showed no mercy, none of these girls got a quick and easy death no matter how annoying their screaming voices projected. He had a sweet passion for abusing their bodies slowly until they were almost unrecognisable.

Growing up in a foster home, no one ever showed him authority so he had no boundaries or rules in his life. He was very much a loner and barely held a conversation with another human being apart from these women. The women he meets are always over the internet; they all had some sort of depressing story; divorced, single, alone, just anyone of them who is desperate for private attention of a good looking man.

The man who is now a man of the shadows, used to be a very handsome gentleman. He was tall, dark haired and his eyes were brown that would make any girl weak at the knees. Many women couldn't believe their luck when he responded to their messages online. He was a God on the internet. The man was simply irresistible.

The killing of these women was probably a cry for help because all he ever wanted was somebody to love, like his mother perhaps. Never in his whole life had he ever met his mother. The poor man was left on the steps of a child care home. That night was very cold and wet which made the people of the foster home wonder how he survived there considering they believed he must have been there for almost 8 hours. All of the other children who he lived with never really spoke to him. The boys never did because they were jealous of how incredibly good looking he was and nothing bad ever happen to that child. The girls tried to talk to him but soon gave up when he refused to speak and most days he locked himself away in his room.

The man in the shadow felt like the world owed him a favour so he wanted to rob the world of all the women who lived. He wasn't far off finding the perfect women to marry. He didn't even look for anyone that suited his needs, although there was one. The irresistible, charming man scanned through the dating forum looking for the next women, when suddenly, a particular female caught his eye. She was nothing special, just a plane Jane, who loved to read and write stories of her own. Her hair was mousy brown and curly, with eyes that were green which shone like an emerald. Every time he has had female attention was because they would be the ones to message him first, however his taste for plane Jane wouldn't go away, so he broke the tradition and messaged her first.

After sending a friendly message, he waited nervously for almost two hours. When three hours went by so slowly, his hands began to sweat and his head was hot with embarrassment and frustration. When he was about to give up she messaged him back apologising for the delay but she couldn't find the right words to reply as this was the first message she ever received. After a week of constant messages, he was getting impatient, so he offered himself to her for an evening of romance. At first she was quite nervous to accept but his soft words of promise on the phone made her fall madly in love. His voice was so sexy; the confidence inside you will want to scream out 'I love you'.

Chapter Two

On the night of the date, he was nervous for once. Taking another person's life didn't cross his mind for almost a week. He believed this girl had changed him even though their bodies have yet to meet. At exactly 7.30pm she knocked on his door. The curls of her hair bounced as she walked through the door and her teeth shone bright through the red painted lips, which matched her not so plain dress. The man's eyes nearly fell out of his head when she appeared in front of him, never has he ever been lost for words. The Plain Jane has stolen his heart.

The evening was perfect, the conversations didn't stop and he couldn't help asking if she wanted to go on another date the following night. Not having to think about it she said yes and from then a relationship started. A whole year flew by and not once did he even need a taste of blood from anyone. This man thought he had changed but one night, she triggered the evil inside of him to come out again.

The Plain Jane was nervous and quite quiet on the phone one evening. The man could sense there was something wrong and asked her to explain. With no intention of telling him face to face she decided they should go their separate ways. A different emotion attacked his insides, causing him to feel pain. His eyes began to leak, but with no real sympathy she simply said he was too full on and everything was going too fast for her. He, the shadow man told her he would change. She replied that it was too late and before she put the phone down, she said to him softly that was she sorry.

The tears and the pain that showed in this man suddenly changed. The love bubble he had been in for too long exploded, and the darkness in his soul was free. Free to play with the souls of women again, but first he was going to find Plain Jane.

Sitting in her bed, reading her book, Plain Jane heard someone at the door. Putting on her dressing gown she headed for the door but before she could get there, her door creaked open. Squeezing tightly onto her book she slowly looked outside the door. Nobody was there. With a sigh of relief she closed the door but as she turned round, he was there. He was so close to her face their noses almost touched. Plain Jane's face turned white and her eyes didn't even blink, they just focused on his. Opening her mouth, not one word came out. He reached in his pocket and pulled out a tiny book of love poems.

He told her that his book was meant to be a present for her but because of what she has done, he reached into his other pocket and pulled out a lighter and began to set alight the book. She was about to scream for help but his cold hand covered her mouth and dropped the burning book. He told her to be quiet and that he had come here to help her get better, to free her from the evil that caused her to become like this. Her forehead wrinkled with confusion, her mouth was free to speak and she asked what he was doing.

He let out a laugh and smiled. Raising his hand he shoved his fingers down her throat, telling her he was pulling out the evil from her soul. Tears fell to the floor and her body wanted her to be sick but he told her if she was he would cut out her heart. Taking what he believed was evil; her throat became free to breathe. She started to cough and her breathing caused her to panic. Making too much noise he took the book from her hands and smacked her round the head causing her to hit her head again on the chair as she fell to the floor.

Plain Jane suddenly opened her eyes to realise she was tied to a chair. As she looked down she could see her clothes were soaked in blood. The room was filled with smoke from the fire, which made it difficult to see him. She suddenly noticed her wrists were cut and she screamed. She tried to turn round but she couldn't see a thing. The smoke filled her lungs, and her coughing got ridiculously out of control, so she started to choke. Then out of nowhere, the backs of her legs were cut and still she couldn't see him. She tried to scream for help but nobody came. The tears from her eyes wiped away the black smoke on her face. Unaware of where he was, his face appeared through the smoke and they were eye level. Breathing through a mask, he watched her suffering. Lifting her top, he raised his cold sharp knife and cut across her chest. Plain Jane's screams got louder and irritating. Looking in her kitchen, he found some tape. Leaving her with one last kiss, he taped her mouth. The blood from her body wouldn't stop, making her body weaker and slowly dying. He freshly cut her wrists again, and licked the blood away, feeding his thirst. Before he left her to die, he cut a piece of her hair and whispered 'I love you', as he headed for the door; he took one last look and closed the door.

In addition to heartache from what his mother did, Plain Jane was added to it. Two very special people that were meant to be in his life hurt him carelessly.

Chapter Three

The shadow man and Elliot's mother share a story quite similar. This being that Elliot's mother Lisa lived in the same foster home as the shadow man from the day she was born. You would think that the opportunity of a brand new baby would excite couples who long for a child but nobody wanted her. It wasn't that she was an ugly baby, it just quite difficult to explain, it was almost like a force field surrounded her and that every time a gushing couple came close, they would suddenly turn weird and refuse. On a massive wall at the foster home were tiny photos of every child that had ever lived there. Every night before Lisa went to sleep she would look at the wall and say goodnight to every single person in the photos, except for one. The one she did not talk to was the picture that had no name that being the shadow man's picture.

One time she did question the people who worked in the foster home what his name was but they all changed the subject and refused to talk about him. Although Lisa did not speak to the picture with no name she always touched his picture and pretended to stroke his beautiful hair.

As Lisa got older she fell in love with her old school boyfriend and now they are married with lovely children, one being Elliot of course. When she said her final goodbye's at the foster home, she took one final look at those pictures and said goodbye. When she got to the picture with no name, she stroked his hair and without anyone looking she took the picture from the frame and put it in one of her boxes.

Before she was about to leave an older person who had worked there since the day Lisa arrived, handed her an old battered black book. Lisa looked puzzled and asked her what it was and she told her that she promised that when Lisa was older she was to give this to her. Not caring what is was she just chucked it in one of her boxes and left her old life to start something new with the one she loved.

Chapter Four

On the night of the killing of his girlfriend, the shadow man drowned his sorrows with a bottle of the finest whisky. Sleeping in his chair in front of the fake fire place, he quickly jumped by the sound of someone knocking on the door. He looked at the clock which said 3.09am, he thought that the batteries had run out but when he looked out the window it was still dark. Could this be an emergency?

He quickly answered the door to find out it was the police, he stared blankly into the distance and froze. He thought that night was going to be how he finally got arrested but instead of cuffing his hands they asked if they could come in. They told in detail of the horror incident occurring with his girlfriend. They started to explain that at her house there had been a really bad fire and they found her body covered in a horrible state. They took her outside to try and revive her and after ten minutes of trying they did so. Taking her to hospital they discovered that she was 8 months pregnant. To the shadow man's horror he asked if there was some kind of mistake and she never even looked pregnant and if she was why didn't she tell him? A shocked look plastered on the shadow man's face. How can this be?

The police officer reassured him that it was the correct person; they carried on with telling him that they had to do an emergency caesarean which has led to the congratulation that the baby girl is ok. However, shortly after the baby was born, his girlfriend died by losing a lot of blood. A baby? He thought, no way in hell was this even true. After the police left his house the shadow man was in panic. He paced up and down the room, not knowing what to feel, was this even a dream? He tried pinching himself but it only proved that this was really happening. Then out of nowhere a plan came to mind.

He headed to the hospital and acted as a doting husband who had just lost his wife to a sicko. With his handsome smile, every nurse fell in love and they all rushed to comfort him in this sad time. Leaving with a few numbers (Of course, they only gave them to him in case he needed some comforting) he took the baby and headed for the door. Driving straight to his old foster home, he kissed the little girl on the head and left her outside and ran. Attached to the baby was a note which simply said 'I'm sorry' and his book which contained her mother's hair inside.

Chapter Five

Lisa and her new husband had a lovely family with a lovely house and a lovely life. Their lives were filled with busy schedules of children and work but Lisa and her husband still remained forever in love just like they did when they first met. When Lisa was pregnant with twins after having two sons already, they decided it was time to get a bigger house as there simply was not enough room for everyone.

Making the final part of their packing complete, Lisa decided to look through her old boxes of childhood memories. Pictures of happy times with other foster children made her smile, but as she looked through more it made her sad to think that every single friend she made in that place soon disappeared to a loving family while she stayed put. Lisa always wondered why nobody bothered with adopting her as part of their family, especially as she was such a good child. Looking through the rest of her stuff made her think of her real parents and who they were. Sadness began to fill up inside and she wanted answers.

Instead of finishing packing, Lisa decided to go back to her foster home, but as soon as she stood up she noticed the black book that one of the workers at the foster home gave her. She picked it up and wiped away the dust. The black leather book still smelt strongly of leather. As she opened it, she quickly jumped with horror and it fell out of her hands. Inside the book she saw clumps of hair of all the women the shadow man had taken. She picked the book back up and looked at each page. Each clump of hair had beside them a name and a reason of what they did to him. As she got to the last page, she stared at the one clump of hair that was stuck in the middle. Next to the hair wrote 'Plain Jane- you will remain forever the one but you broke my heart' a tear from Lisa's eye fell silently down her face. Poor man, she thought, the love of his life broke his heart so he killed her. Such tragedy and sorrow. Wondering what this man was like, she quickly had a thought as to why she was given this book to begin with.

When she got to the foster home she smiled because coming back was like visiting home. Before she knocked on the door there was a very old lady walking out. When she looked up and saw Lisa, she knew exactly who she was and smiled. The fragile old lady was the only person who knew Lisa ever since she was born so she felt like Lisa was her daughter. They went in the house and talked over a cup of tea and biscuits. When Lisa finally had the courage, she asked why she was given the black book. The fragile old lady took a deep breath and sighed. 'Oh' she said. She was hoping to be long gone before Lisa ever asked her what it was. Lisa looked concerned and worried as to why this book was such a secret. The old lady started by telling her this:

"Ever since you were bought to me, I wouldn't let any of the other staff here really look after you; I felt a connection, a bond. I wasn't really sure how to describe it but it felt like love. When I picked you up from the door step you weren't crying you were just staring at me with those big eyes and I knew you were special. With you was a piece of paper saying 'I'm sorry' and this black book. I admit I did look inside the book but I never quite understood why. Many months after you arrived here you had a visitor. When this visitor arrived it turned out to be your father. He was a very handsome man I can tell you that. But he looked very familiar. I later learned that your mother had tragically died in a fire while she was carrying you and your father was in such a shock that you even existed he didn't even know a thing about having a child. Although he visited you many times his face grew more familiar to me. When I realised who he was, he disappeared."

Lisa was speechless she didn't even know what to say. Why didn't anyone say anything before? Lisa asked the lady how she knew who he was and she said:

"Your father used to live here with me when he was younger. I remember when I first started working here I always thought he was going to be such a lady's man. I can show you a picture if you like"

Lisa nodded, and as the old lady got up Lisa followed her to the hallway where it had all the pictures of every child that lived here. As she looked for his face, she noticed a gap on the wall of where his picture once was. The little old lady apologised and said that it used to be there. Lisa gulped and realised that the picture of the boy with no name that she took those years ago was her father. Realising this, Lisa ran out outside and ran home.

When she returned to her house she took the picture from the box and locked herself in the bathroom. Sitting behind the door on the floor she just stared into the picture.

Chapter Six

After the birth of Lisa's twin daughters she decided to find out somehow where her father was. She tried every nursing home, hospitals, jut anywhere in the area. She didn't even know how old he was or if he was alive and after a while of having no luck she got herself so stressed all because she wanted to find out so badly. Over a month of trying to find him she was going to give up until she suddenly had a thought. Looking through his black leather book with all these women's names and hair she thought that maybe he had been arrested for this?

Embarrassingly she searched through the phone book finding a number for all the prisons that were not that far. In total she had four. Not knowing his actual name she tried to give as much information as she could about him, describing him just like the lady at the foster home did. With three tries she began to feel silly but with one last number left she thought why not call it. The person down the telephone let out a silent pause and with a bit of hesitation the woman down the phone said she thinks she has the right person. With that Lisa got herself ready and thought it was about time she met her father.

Wearing a black pencil skirt, white top and a black blazer, she finally felt ready. Elliot, her eldest child was summoned to babysit his new-born sisters. Not giving anything away, Lisa said she was going to visit an old friend and not knowing any different Elliot accepted the job.

Pulling up to the prison, her hands were glued to the steering wheel. The nervous feeling you get waiting for a dentist appointment is exactly how she felt. All these different questions were flying through her mind and not one seemed suitable to start with. Staring straight ahead she felt her eyes stinging and a different thought popped into her mind: 'what if he doesn't want to speak to me?' knowing that he has clearly done something terrible she still has that horrible heart ache feeling of wondering whether she is going to be rejected again.

With her hands trembling she took a deep breath, closed her eyes and breathed back out again. She opened the door and made her way to the front door. For the first time in her life, Lisa was going to meet the man that never bothered to keep in contact with her. Lisa was about to meet her father.

As she waited at a table for him to show his face, she looked around the room at the other people who have come to visit their loved ones, family members or friends. Lisa felt warmth inside her knowing that he accepted the offer of her meeting.

Suddenly a loud noise of the bell rang, echoing the room causing ringing in her ears. This was a sign that the prisoners were coming out. Her heart began to beat so loud she thought others could hear. Her palms began to sweat and her head suddenly got hotter. With all the other prisoners sat at the tables, hers was remained empty. Then the door opened.

Chapter Seven

The night the shadow man stopped seeing his little girl was when the lady at the foster home realised who he was. Feeling a little ashamed that he never visited when he left the home he decided to make a run for it. Sacrificing the chance to see his little girl all because they recognised him seemed a little harsh, but in fact it was because he used to date one of the girls at the home until her hair was added to his little black book. With the black book also now belonging to his daughter, there was no doubt in his mind that all the workers at the care home have seen inside the book.

Inside the shadows man's chest lays a heart which used to be black apart from now, right at the bottom of his heart is love. Love for his little girl. With the love he had from the mother of his child he didn't think any other kind of love was possible. The love for his child was something he didn't even know how to describe. He felt that with this love he had to protect her but with others having a chance of knowing his secret he could no longer do that.

As nights went by he began to struggle and felt his insides hurting and he had a feeling you get when you miss someone. He thought he could cope with it but as much of a horrible man he was, he just couldn't. The shadow man went to the foster home and was about to knock on the door but something inside him stopped him from doing it, so instead he looked through the sitting room window and saw her sitting on the floor watching TV with some of the other children. The shadow man began to feel happy again. Little Lisa must of felt a presence of somebody watching her as she turned and looked at the window and saw him watching her. The shadow man waved his arms about to signal to her to be quiet and instead of getting up to see him she just smiled then carried on watching the TV.

A whole month of nothing to do now that he believed his secret could be out in the open he thought he could change to be a better man so that maybe one day in the future he could finally live with his little girl and start afresh. The once professional killer in his own right suddenly changed from killing innocent women to falling in love and having a child. But once a killer, there's no doubt he will always be a killer. Just one little nudge of annoyance or constant pestering and he will be right back to being a cold blooded killer. The emptiness he felt of not seeing his little girl anymore began to anger him so he decided it was time to start a new chapter of killings with a new book.

A girl of many was the last one to fill his second book. When he went back to her place, she poured him a glass of blood red wine and sat so close to him on the sofa, she may as well of sat on his lap. With the constant chat of her beloved cat he could feel his patience wearing thin. Inside his body he suddenly snapped, but before the rest of his body showed his anger he finished his glass of wine and stood up. The pretty blonde, asked him what he was doing and he simply asked which way it was to her bathroom. Reading mixed signals, she headed for the bedroom while he was in the bathroom preparing her death. He grabbed various medication bottles from his jacket pocket and poured a mixture in his hand. As she was waiting in the bedroom he headed to the kitchen and made them both another drink of red wine, with hers adding the mixture of drugs. Watching the drugs melt he plastered a smile across his face and headed to the bedroom.

Downing the glass of wine, she started to sway as though she was dizzy from too much drink when in fact it was the drugs. Trying to stand up she instead fell to the floor hitting her head on the hard wooden floor. Tying her to a chair, the shadow man suddenly went into a daze of remembrance of the day he tied plane Jane up. The shadow man just wanted to run away from this but he knew he couldn't as she may say something to the police when she wakes up. Smacking his head with his hand, he agreed to go through with it, so he reached into his other jacket pocket and pulled out a needle.

Injecting air into the needle he stabbed her arm and injected her vein with air. Waiting to see if she dies, he sat patiently on her bed. Checking her pulse every half an hour and still he felt her alive. Deciding that it was taking too long he headed for the kitchen to get the biggest knife she had. On returning to her room he noticed she was awake. Still drowsy she tried to ask what was going on but the shadow man said nothing but told her to shush. Instead she started to get louder and louder until he stabbed her in the leg but still not keeping her mouth shut she screamed to be heard. He raised his arm again and repeatedly stabbed her in the chest until the room was silent.

Dropping the knife he fell the floor and cried. He reached for his phone and called 999. The almighty shadow man began to confess he killed a woman and that if they didn't hurry he would disappear only to continue with his quest.

Within five minutes sirens of police cars and ambulances deafened the whole street. The police banged down the front door and grabbed the shadow man. When they took him outside crowds of people gathered and stared at the beautiful killer that stood before them. With evidence of the second black book they had enough to send him to prison forever.

Chapter Eight

Serving over 20 years of his sentence the shadow man got him a bit of reputation in the prison and soon became the leader inside the prison. Only the stupid and new prisoners would dare to question his authority, and when they did, they soon had their lives taken from them. Knowing he would never leave and having being put on the list for death row, he didn't care whether more people's lives were taken as he was already dead in his own way.

With his name never known to anybody the prison guards and prisoners started to call him the shadow man. The reason for this was because the police who recorded the murders of all these women never figured out who it was so to them it was a man in the shadows hence the shadow man.

When the shadow man heard the news that his daughter wanted to visit, all those feelings he felt years ago came flooding back and he remembered what love felt like again. He pictured her little face through the window and could see her smiling. He wondered why she is bothering with him after leaving her all those years ago. But he felt so grateful that she has given him the opportunity to explain himself finally.

The day of the visit he sat nervously in his cell. Other prisoners began to notice a change in the shadow man. They thought that maybe he had gone a little soft so they tried to take advantage but even though his daughters face was in his mind he still happily hurt those who stood in his way.

When the prison bell finally rang he made his way to the meeting room. He was worried of what sort of person she may think he was and started to have these doubt of her hating him. The meeting room door opened and he suddenly panicked and moved out of the queue and headed back into his cell. A prison guard asked what he was doing and the shadow man said he didn't know what to do.

With everyone else in the waiting room he paced up and down the hall wondering whether he should meet his daughter or not. Closing his eyes he pictured his little girls face and smiled. Pushing out all of the hate he usually feels inside he replaced it with the love he had for his daughter. He opened his eyes and without thinking he walked straight through the door and into the meeting room.

He searched the room for the table with an empty chair, when he found the one table in the back his eyes met a stranger. There in front of the shadow man was little Lisa all grown up. Heading for the table Lisa just sat there staring straight into his eyes, not even blinking.

At first when the shadow man sat down, they both looked at each other waiting for one another to speak. After 5 minutes of silence he broke the peace and began to speak. His mouth opened and the words that came out of his mouth and then the words that came out of her mouth it was as if they were a normal family who meet every Sunday for a roast dinner. Although she may not have entirely forgiven him for the death of her mother and the fact he abandoned her, she put all of that aside just to be with the one man she so longed to be with.

With so much to say to each other, not once did the shadow truly explain as to who he really was or what he had done. Lisa didn't really want to know what happened as she just wanted to spend as much time with him before it was his time to go.

Visiting him every two weeks for three months, Lisa decided he was ready to meet his grandchildren. She knew she would have a lot of explaining to do, especially to Elliot as he was the only one who was old enough to really understand what was going on. But despite having to do that she felt she owed it to her children to meet their grandfather at least once while he was alive.

The following two weeks went by and Monday was the day that Lisa's children were going to meet the shadow man. When they arrived at the front of the prison, the whole family was silent. Not even the twins let out a little moan or cry. When she got to the front desk the lady behind it had a puzzling look on her face when Lisa said who she was here to meet. The lady behind the desk pulled her to one side and told her that she was unable to visit the shadow man today because it was the day he was going to be electrocuted. With the word electrocuted repeating in her mind she panicked and screamed that she must see him first, but the lady said it would be too late as they were preparing for him at this very second. Lisa fell to the floor and screamed as loud as she could for her father. Tears fell from her face and her two little twins began to scream and cry too. The lady put her arms around Lisa and sympathised with her but Lisa pushed her away. Wiping away her smudged mascara, she took her children home.

That very evening Elliot sat with his mother on the sofa, not saying a single word. Wanting to find out who this man was, Elliot made it his mission the following day to head to the prison to ask questions.

Chapter Nine

Tuesday morning arrived and Elliot took the bus to the prison to where the shadow man lived. Upon arrival the same lady as yesterday was sitting behind the desk, typing away. When she noticed Elliot she asked how she could help and that's when Elliot learnt the truth.

The shadow man was still alive. The electrocution didn't work and the shadow man believed that when it started and he felt himself frothing at the mouth he managed to survive because he heard his little girl Lisa scream for him through the walls.

The lady behind the desk asked if he would like to visit the shadow man. Elliot wasn't sure whether his mother would want him to but he accepted anyway. Waiting at the very same table his mother was when she met him; he waited nervously with the other people in the room. When the bell rang loudly the prisoners came out the door one by one. When the shadow man approached Elliot's table, Elliot quickly stood up holding his hand out so the shadow man could shake it. The shadow man stood there staring at Elliot and seeing how similar he is to Elliot when he was the same age. Instead of the shadow man shaking his hand he grabbed Elliot and hugged him tightly.

When they sat down to talk the connection between the two of them was unreal. Elliot felt as though some sort of power was dancing in his body. Finding out that the shadow man was his granddad, he started to ask more questions as to where his grandma was and why he was in here. The shadow man kept his cool and said that this subject was something his mother should answer and he shouldn't worry. After agreeing to meet him again next time with the rest of the family, Elliot said goodbye and rushed home to tell his mother the news. At first she didn't believe him and told him he was cruel for making such a thing up but when he started describing him, her heart sank to her belly button. She couldn't believe that he was still alive.

The next visit to the prison quickly came back around and Lisa took all the children again for another try, this time she bought her husband along after some persuasion. Although he was happy that she finally found a piece to her missing puzzle he still worried for her because when the time comes for him to be killed yet another time she is going to be devastated.

When the shadow man entered the visiting room he had never felt so loved. A warm glow filled his face and his heart felt different after every beat. All these people were here to see him and nobody else and because of that all of the bad things he did had disappeared. Meeting the rest of the family, every single person he hugged he fell in love just like he did when he saw little Lisa's face.

When the time was up for them to leave the shadow man asked Lisa if he could speak to her quickly in private. He told her that this may be the last time he will ever see her as there are talks that his execution was going to happen very soon. With her eyes starting to fill up he told he not to cry in front of her family as they will know something is wrong. He handed her an envelope and told her not to open it until he had left this world. She took it and put it in her coat pocket. Before she left he told her how much he loved her and how much he loved her family and he finally thanked her for making his wish come true. With maybe a last goodbye hug it was time to leave. As the shadow man stood there watching her walk away, one single tear fell from this man's body. Who could ever believe that his very own family could melt this evil man's heart?

After that day Lisa waited anxiously for a call from the prison telling her of his time to leave but as a week went by the rest of the minutes in the days she dreaded. When it got to 1 week and six days she actually believed that the following day she was going to be able to see her father again. However at 6pm that night the telephone rang and it was the lady that sat behind the desk at the prison. She told Lisa that unfortunately her father was going to be given a new lethal injection the following day considering as the electrocution did not work. She said that she and whoever she wanted was allowed to watch behind a window. Trying not to cry Lisa wanted to see her father even if it meant to watch him die.

Chapter Ten

Dressed in black from head to toe, Lisa was ready to see her father one last time. Leaving her husband and her children behind she headed for the long dreaded drive across town. The closer she got to the prison the more real she realised the situation. Not long ago she believed that she didn't have a father that was alive, but after finding him and bonding with him she finds out so soon that he was to be taken away from her was so confusingly heart-breaking.

After parking in a space she followed a group of people into a room. All these people who surrounded her were the people who wanted him dead and wanted to make sure he died this time. As everyone took a seat, Lisa quickly pushed her way through to have a seat right at the front. On the other side of the glass the shadow man entered the room with his hands behind his back. When he took his seat he looked at the glass and stared at Lisa. He gave her a quick smile but she did not return the smile back in case anyone suspected who she was. Everyone in the room was the families of the victims her father had killed. Searching the room she did wonder whether anyone was related or knew her mother but she daren't ask in case they started asking questions back.

When the injection was given to the shadow man everyone in the room cheered with happiness and excitement. Lisa just sat there as still as can be with her eyes focused on her father. As he slowly died, no emotion showed on her face, nothing.

As Lisa sat in a crowded room,

Behind thick glass she knew her father's doom,

No tears did fall from her sweet face,

No emotion showed but her heart did race,

Touching the glass she stared into his eyes,

All the badness disappeared; the killing, the pain, the bad, the lies,

His body slumped on the chair with no life left at all,

Lisa's secret must be hidden, but the floor is where she wanted to fall,

All these strangers with smiles and a feel of relief,

Lisa thought they were nothing but a thief,

Who individually took away her father's life,

She felt she could end each of them with a knife,

She felt her chest explode like water bursting a pipe,

Her father was gone but his memory she will never wipe,

The shadow man killed these women for pleasure,

Then cut their hair and kept as treasure,

Lisa lost her father; parents she had none,

Does she mourn her loss? Or does her taste for her father's revenge just begun?

Chapter Eleven

Arriving home, Lisa wanted to do nothing but sit in her bed all day with no distraction. With her husband not having experienced such a terrible loss himself he did his best to help her. He took all the children away for the day so she could be free to do as she pleased. Elliot began to start asking his dad questions but with his father saying nothing Elliot thought of his own reasons as to this secrecy. At first he thought it was something he did wrong but the more of he thought about it he finally realised it was something to do with the shadow man, his granddad. When Elliot asked his dad if there was something wrong with his granddad he continued to say nothing but the look in his eyes confessed it all.

At home, Lisa rummaged through her things trying to find that picture of her father from when he was younger but she couldn't find it anywhere. What she did find however, was the envelope her father gave her. She sat there on her bed staring at the scruffy envelope and wondering whether she wanted to open it and read the whole truth.

Still clutching hold of the envelope Lisa had fallen asleep. Her dreams were terrible, she kept seeing her father being killed in viscous ways by the people who watched him die that day and as the dreams went on the people who were killing her father started to try and kill her.

Lisa found herself running away in her dream until she fell of the earth and woke up. Covered in sweat she saw the envelope in her hand and she quickly put on a light and opened it.

The confession letter

To my baby girl who I remember so small and cute,

My life before you I had always kept mute,

Before I confess, I wanted you to know,

When you were little I didn't want to let you go,

But the life I lived was not cut out for you,

You and your mother I loved you two,

But my wicked ways just wanted me more,

I am sorry that these things may shock your core,

These things I did weren't because of you and your mum,

But forgive me please if these things make you numb,

My little girl who grew so wonderful and bright,

Your husband and children I loved them alright,

But when things get hard in life just remember to always fight,

I will be watching out for you every single night,

When I was young I had no-one who loved me,

The people at the foster home just let me be,

So I went on my way and chose a life of bad,

Because inside, all that was left was sad,

I killed a lot of women as your probably know,

At the end of each date their home is where they didn't go,

Each girl was special with their lives taken away,

They were each killed in a different way,

When I first met your mum was when I felt love,

It was like the heaven gave me an angel from up above,

But she didn't love me as much as I did her,

Not being with me is what she would prefer,

So a part of my list was where she was to go,

She was pregnant at that time but then I didn't know,

I thought it was over until I learnt of you,

My heart was no longer left in two,

But keeping you away from the danger of what I was,

I hope you understand why and don't need a because,

My sins I am confessing only to you,

Telling you this is making me feel blue,

The shadow man is me and it's who I am,

But keeping you safe I sure did give a damn,

You're my precious, my one, my little girl,

I love you always and forever my special pearl.

Goodbye my child I can longer pretend,

The shadow man's life has gone and this is the end.

I love you, daddy. Xo

CPSIA information can be obtained at www.ICGtesting.com
Printed in the USA
LVOW06*2002290414

383731LV00011B/262/P

9 781291 787481